PRE-B⚙T™ LEARNS NOT TO HURT

Story by Rod Lowe
Illustrations by Gatto

*To my loving wife and family who've been the biggest support to me,
and the many wonderful kids that have inspired
me to write this series.*

Printed in China

First Printing, 2018
ISBN 978-0-9970012-1-1

Pre-Bot™
Groton, MA 01450

www.Pre-Bot.com

Meet Timmy. This is his first robot.

His name is Pre-Bot. Timmy's parents bought him as a surprise.

Timmy was so excited! Right away he ripped open the packaging and asked his mom to read the instructions for him.

"Pre-Bot learns by copying your example," Timmy's mom said. "So you'll need to set a good one."

"An example is something that a person tries to imitate. Timmy, you can be an example by what you do or say. If you're a good example, then Pre-Bot will be a good robot," explained his mom.

As Pre-Bot powered up, Timmy's mom said, "I'll leave you with Pre-Bot now, so you can both have fun and play."

Pre-Bot turned his head and started to watch Timmy's every move.

"What are you doing?" asked Pre-Bot.

"I'm laughing, Pre-Bot! People laugh when they're happy," explained Timmy.

"Why are you happy?" asked Pre-Bot.

"It's because of you Pre-Bot. You make me feel good, and I laugh when I feel good," said Timmy.

Pre-Bot started to laugh and said, "Then I am happy too."

Timmy's little brother Tommy
came into the room and asked,
"Is that a Pre-Bot?"

"Yes, but he's not a toy
for babies!" Timmy teased.

"Anyway, you already have your baby toy, Chookum. If you like Pre-Bot so much, then I guess you won't need Chookum anymore!" Timmy teased.

Timmy then grabbed Chookum out of Tommy's arms.

"Timmy, Chookum is mine! Give him back!" screamed Tommy.

"Calm down, Tom-Tom," Timmy said playfully. "I'm not going to hurt him. I'm just going to flush him down the toilet!"

Then Timmy pushed his brother so hard, that he fell and hit his head!

"MOM!" screamed
Tommy uncontrollably.

"Timmy! Why would you pick on Tommy like that? Don't you see he's crying?" scolded his mom.

"Tell him you're sorry and then go to your room!
You need to think about what you've done!
And no dessert!"

"Mom doesn't understand that I was just playing with Tommy!" Timmy explained to Pre-Bot. "Sometimes parents just don't understand."

"So you have fun playing this way?" asked Pre-Bot.

"Yes, it's fun," answered Timmy. "Now let's get ready for bed, before I get into trouble again."

Timmy decided to read his favorite book to Pre-bot, and then they both fell asleep.

10 things a T-REX CAN'T DO.

The next day
Timmy told Pre-Bot,
"Be good, Pre-Bot.
Please prove to my mom that
I've set a good example for you!"

At home, everyone seemed to have something to do, except
for Pre-Bot. Pre-Bot wanted to have something to do, too!

Pre-Bot had an idea!
He'd play the game
Timmy taught him,
with the family pets!

He started by sneaking
up on Sheba the cat
and then...

SNAP! Pre-Bot pinched the cat!

"RAWRRR!" meowed Sheba, as
she jumped high in the air.

Pre-Bot didn't want to get caught,
so he ran away as fast as he could!

He then did the same to Ruff the dog, Squeaks
the hamster, and even tried to pinch Bentley the fish!

Timmy finally came home and went to his
room to see Pre-Bot. Timmy reached
out to pick him up, but to
his surprise...

SNAP! Pre-Bot turned around and pinched him!

"Pre-Bot, that really hurt!" exclaimed Timmy. "If you do that again, I won't play with you!"

"But you hurt Tommy and that was fun, right?" asked Pre-Bot.

Timmy sighed and thought
to himself, "Pre-Bot is right. Tommy
wasn't having fun when I was teasing him."

Timmy walked over to Tommy
and apologized for hurting him.

Pre-Bot decided to show
all the pets that he
was sorry too.

He brought milk to Sheba the cat;

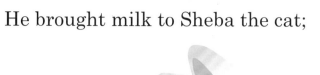

gave cheese to
Squeaks the hamster;

gave Ruff the dog a nice back rub;

and cleaned the
tank of Bentley the fish.

Timmy was
proud to be able
to teach Pre-Bot
such a good lesson.

"Only bullies
like hurting people
for fun" said Timmy.

"Then I never want to
be known as a bully!"
exclaimed Pre-Bot.

"Good, Pre-Bot! Now let's go race outside! That's a game I can teach you where no one needs to get hurt!" said Timmy.

Pre-Bot smiled, "You are a good example Timmy. I am happy, that you are my teacher."

The End